British Library Cataloguing in Publication Data
Bowen, Elizabeth P.
  Coop
  I. Title
  823'.914(J)   PZ7

  ISBN 0-340-32673-5

First published 1984

Published by Hodder & Stoughton Children's Books
a division of Hodder & Stoughton Ltd, Mill Road,
Dunton Green, Sevenoaks, Kent TN13 2YJ

Designed by Graham Marks

Printed in Hong Kong by Colorcraft Ltd.

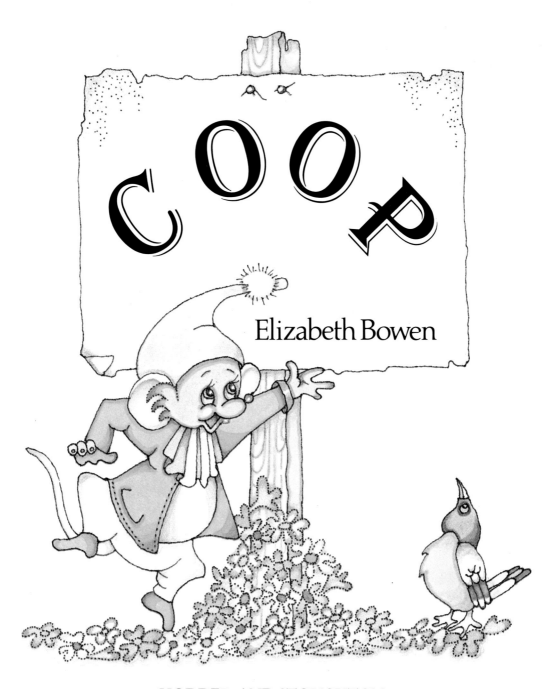

COOP

Elizabeth Bowen

HODDER AND STOUGHTON
LONDON SYDNEY AUCKLAND TORONTO

Once, in a deep hollow of a beech tree, lived a tiny mouse.

Alone.

His parents had long since left him to fend for himself. 'There is nothing to him!' they exclaimed to each other. 'There is really nothing special about him at all; do not give him another thought!'

And so saying they left without a backward glance.

Quite soon he realised he must stay where he was for some time. It was too cold out of doors; snow flakes fell from the sky like feathers, and thin fingers of ice sealed over the hard surface of the ground, but although he busied himself as best he could, lining the roof with moss, filling the cracks and crannies with bracken to keep out the icy winds, he grew daily more sad and lonely.

'Oh! It is so lonely here!' he thought. 'This is no life for me! Why, I have no proper home, no food and no friends. In fact, I haven't even a name!'

Time passed; but one day he felt a strange restlessness all about him, and realised that he must now leave the safety of his home, and explore the broad world. 'I think I will take my chance, and go!' he said, and without more ado he packed his few possessions in a handkerchief, and set forth.

Up the grassy bank he scrambled and saw that the country looked lovely: the carpet of snow had been replaced by a carpet of flowers.

It was Spring!

'This is fine!' he said to himself. 'This has been well worth waiting for!' and he rolled over and over in the warm grass, the sun full on his face, crying 'Oh my! Oh my!' from sheer happiness. It all seemed too good to be true!

Rambling along meadow paths hidden by long grasses he spied a farmyard, where, looking for all the world like a dolls' house, stood a little hen coop. Lazy smoke billowed from its chimney, snowdrops dipped on to its roof, and he thought what a fine home this would make for him. Tip-toeing cautiously forward, he whispered:

'Little House, little House, are *you* the home for me?'

And nobody answered.

A hen was scratching about in the yard picking grain, but she was so busy that she did not even look round, so quickly he scurried up the steps, heart thumping, and crept into a dark corner.

'Why, it might have been made just for me!' he thought, and lay back, snug and secure, in the warmth of the straw.

Meanwhile, the Rooster strutted and crowed, well aware of his
wonderful tail and golden eyes. He lifted his head high and crowed:
'Cock-a-doodle-do!

Fat Hen will lay for you!'

Obediently, Fat Hen put on her bonnet, and carefully picked her way
over to the splendid velvet cushion which was prepared for her in the
shade of a willow tree. Rooster kept a watchful eye, and scoured the
yard for intruders while Fat Hen was nesting, but all he could see was
the farmer humping sacks of grain by the barn, so all was well. He did
not notice the quiet mouse that had crept down to see what all the
clucking and fussing coming from Fat Hen was about. Believe it or not,
Mouse had never, in all his life, seen a baby chick hatched! He listened,
astonished, to the peeping calls from the egg, and then, 'Peep-peep!' said
the little one more loudly, and out it tumbled!

Rooster was alerted by the shuffling noise such as only mice make, and flew in a terrible temper, trying to catch at the seat of poor Mouse's trousers.

'I'll get you yet!' he stormed, but when he saw the little animal take a huge head-first dive into the empty shell, he was very *very* angry, and rushed at him with flapping wings and neck outstretched, furiously hissing.

In desperation, the egg wobbled into an upright position, and staggered across the yard, leaving a trail of small grey footprints. All the creatures of the farmyard stopped to stare. They couldn't believe their eyes.

'Look at that egg walking about!' they shouted excitedly, and they heard a pitiful little voice reply: 'Please, oh please, who will help me?' from within the shell.

'Not I!' shouted the farmer, waving his fork.
And he came RUNNING...
'Not I!' shouted the farmer's wife, shaking her broom.
And she came RUNNING...
'Not I!' screeched the Rooster.
And he came RUNNING...
'Not I!' cheeped the little chick.
And he *tried* to come RUNNING...

The whole world seemed to be running now, closing in on him, and in a panic, Mouse too began to run. He ran up against things — BUMP! — straight into a great plant pot; he fell over things — THUMP! — overturning a bag of grain; and he dodged round things, until he found himself flying through the air in a great arc. The whole world suddenly turned upside down, and when it eventually stopped spinning, he found

he had landed in a soft cushion of ferns outside the farmyard boundary.

Still, from the yard, Rooster was not to be put off, and was heard screeching:

'Keep away from my COOP! Do you hear me? It's *my* COOP,' but just then a strong breeze came by, and all that Mouse could hear was COOP... COOP echoing over the wind.

'That's it!' he shouted. 'That is it, for sure! I have a name —
COOP! It has a certain ring about it. COOP is special, and it's *me*!'

He swelled with pride, and with a leap of the heart, he remembered
too that he was free. Free! He stood up, shook himself, and, looking
neither to right nor to left, set off at a great pace down the lane which
seemed to be beckoning to him. It lead straight into a meadow where
flowers grew, and he heard...

Click-click; clack-clack; click-click.

...and he saw an old woman, quietly knitting, tending her sheep.
She looked up at him with bright little button eyes.

'A fine morning, Ma'am!' he called as he drew level with her.

'Indeed it is, Coop! And you have taken your time getting here, I
must say!'

Before the astonished Coop could ask how she knew his name, she went on:

'You have been expected for some time, so hurry! Hurry! You have not a moment to lose. Your future is waiting on the far side of the hedgerow, you can depend upon it!' And with a strange smile she went back to her knitting, click-clack, click-clack, click-clack.

Through the hedgerow he scrambled, nearly tripping over a young dog who was sitting forlornly by a carpet bag. 'Hullo, Coop!' said the dog, shyly. 'I have been expecting you. My name is Hubble,' he added, by way of explanation.

Then something happened that was the most exciting thing that had happened to Coop all day, or all his life, for that matter. The carpet bag started to glow with a beautiful orange-red luminous light, brilliant, and yet gentle on the eyes, and suddenly it spoke. The voice was deep, and kind.

'Now, heed what I say to you.'

Hubble's teeth started to chatter in fright, he really was a most timid dog, but the bag went on:

'I have magic powers. First, plunge your hands deep inside me, for there you will find your third friend, one who is to be with you on the long adventure that lies ahead.'

Reluctantly, Coop put his hand deep down into the bag, and drew out a sweet, small rag doll, looking very pale and unhappy, with a badly torn leg which hung limply across Coop's arm.

'Hullo, Coop! Hullo Hubble,' she whispered, 'I am Pol-dol; but you are only just in time for I am in so much pain I think I shall surely die!' A large tear ran down her face.

Coop could not even bear the thought that he should so soon lose his new friend so again he reached in the bag and found a needle, a reel of stout thread, and a tiny pair of silver scissors. Hubble took Pol-dol's head in his mouth, supporting her poor leg on a toadstool, whilst Coop sewed busily. For such a young dog he really had the most gentle of mouths, and although she made little moaning noises as Coop stitched, she managed a weak smile of thanks as they laid her back in a nest of tender green leaves.

'Coop you are wonderful,' said Hubble in admiration.

Coop tried to look modest, but the bag spoke again:

'Time passes, and will never return. Seize the moment, magic is not offered to many! You have been chosen, so heed the Call, I beg you. First, you must all rest; take the shawl that lies within me, lie down next to Pol-dol, cover yourselves, and wait!'

Coop lay between them and carefully placed the lacy shawl over them as he was bid. He recognised it as the one he had seen the old woman with the sheep knitting. He was trying to understand it, to bring some order to it all, when Pol-dol spoke:

'I am frightened, Coop,' she said in a small voice.

'And *I* am frightened too!' added Hubble. He was deeply ashamed of this, but he could not change his nature: timid is timid.

Coop looked at them gravely.

'We must be careful,' he warned. 'There are strange creatures in the forest, so we must stay close together. In that way we will be safe.'

They whispered, because there might be wolves — there *could* be wolves, behind each tree, then Coop covered each of them with his arms, wishing he felt as brave as his friends thought him to be.

Suddenly they saw a sparkling shower of small stars, orange and scarlet, spill forth from Carpet Bag. A great hush fell over them as the brilliant skein flowed gently down, spreading over the shawl to form a second coverlet, and on the wind came the sweetest lullaby imaginable.

They smiled as they slept.

By early light, Carpet Bag awoke them. 'Time passes!' he said. 'The world is full of adventures and I intend to see them all! Will you journey with me?'

Coop looked at Hubble...

...Hubble looked at Pol-dol...

...Pol-dol looked at Bag.

Back came the answer:

'We will! We will!'

And they did...just like that!